# waiting for PUMPSIE

Barry Wittenstein

*Illustrated by* London Ladd

ini Charlesbridge

*For Anne and Sam. And in memory of poet and Harpur College creative-writing instructor Robert Pawlikowski, who lives within these words.*

*—B. W.*

*To my mother, Victoria.*

*—L. L.*

Published by Charlesbridge
85 Main Street, Watertown, MA 02472 • (617) 926-0329 • www.charlesbridge.com

**Library of Congress Cataloging-in-Publication Data**
Names: Wittenstein, Barry, author. | Ladd, London, illustrator.
Title: Waiting for Pumpsie / Barry Wittenstein; illustrated by London Ladd.
Description: Watertown, MA: Charlesbridge, [2017] | Summary: In 1959 Bernard is a young
   Red Sox fan, troubled by the lack of black players in Major League Baseball, especially as
   there are none at all on his favorite team—but change is coming in the form of a rookie
   named Pumpsie Green. | Includes bibliographical references.
Identifiers: LCCN 2016013776 | ISBN 9781580895453 (reinforced for library use)
   | ISBN 9781607349495 (ebook) | ISBN 9781607349501 (ebook pdf)
Subjects: LCSH: Green, Pumpsie, 1933– Juvenile fiction. | Boston Red Sox (Baseball team)—
   History—Juvenile fiction. | African American baseball players—Juvenile fiction.
   | Discrimination in sports—United States—History—Juvenile fiction. | Baseball—United
   States—History—Juvenile fiction. | African American families—Juvenile fiction. | Boston
   (Mass.)—History—20th century—Juvenile fiction. | CYAC: Green, Pumpsie, 1933– Fiction.
   | Boston Red Sox (Baseball team)—Fiction. | Baseball—Fiction. | Discrimination—Fiction.
   | African Americans—Fiction. | Boston (Mass.)—History—20th century—Fiction.
Classification: LCC PZ7.1.W6 Wai 2017 | DDC 813.6 [E]—dc23
LC record available at https://lccn.loc.gov/2016013776

Printed in China
(hc) 10 9 8 7 6 5 4 3 2 1

Illustrations done in acrylic paint with touches of
colored pencil on illustration board
Display type set in Block Berthold by Berthold
Types Limited; text type set in Berkeley Oldstyle
   by Adobe Systems Incorporated
      Color separations by Colourscan Print Co Pte
      Ltd, Singapore
         Printed by 1010 Printing International
         Limited in Huizhou, Guangdong, China
         Production supervision by
            Brian G. Walker
            Designed by Diane M. Earley

**I'm Bernard**, and I'm crazy, crazy, crazy
about the Red Sox. Everybody in Boston is.
It's just something you get born into.
We're lucky, I guess.

We always want the Sox to win. But Mama says we gotta root for all the colored players, no matter what team they're on.

"How come the Giants got Willie Mays, and Jackie Robinson retired from the Dodgers, but we still don't have a Negro player?" I ask Papa.

"That's a good question," Papa says. "It's an excellent question."

Every year we go to a game at Fenway Park.
There's no place in the whole world like it. Men with
funny hats and aprons yell, "Get your Cracker Jack!"
The left-field wall even has a name—the Green
Monster. I'm not kidding.

Last year we saw the Sox play the Yankees. Papa complained that they had only one Negro, but I said, "It's one more than we got."

That player, Elston Howard, hit a single to put the Yanks up one to nothing in the second inning. My sister, Lisa, and I jumped up and screamed.

Two men behind us yelled, "Sit down and shut up!"

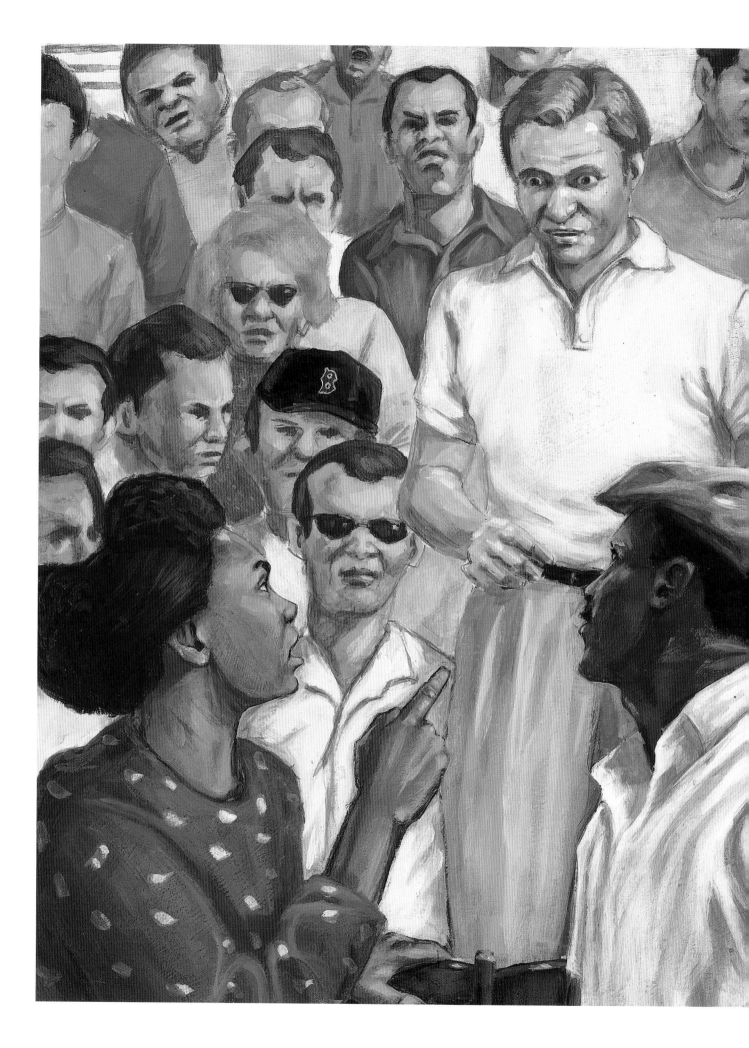

Mama and Papa spun around real fast. One man said a bad word. Mama pointed a finger in his face. "Who do you think you're talking to?" she said.

Then a policeman came over. He said, "You people need to learn how to behave."

He said it to us!

I don't ask Mama and Papa anymore why more colored people don't come to Fenway. I'm old enough now to know.

"Change is coming real soon," Mama said, like she could see the future.

"Is she right?" I asked Papa.

He laughed. "Your mama's always right!"

Then we all laughed, especially Mama.

Besides, the Celtics already got Negro stars Bill Russell and K. C. Jones. Even the Bruins, our hockey team, have a colored player. So why not the Sox?

During spring training we hear about this Negro in the minor leagues, Pumpsie Green. What a great name! Papa says he's the best rookie. Every Sunday I pray for him to make the lineup. Opening day is almost here.

Maybe I don't pray hard enough, 'cause at the last minute they tell him, "Sorry, Pumps. You're not ready."

"Makes no sense," Papa says, shaking his head. "The owner doesn't want colored players on his team. This proves it."

"I don't think it'll ever happen," I say.

Papa's big arms pull me in. "We waited this long, Bernard. What's a little longer?"

Days turn into weeks. Weeks turn into months. The Sox are dropping like a rock into last place.

Papa's newspaper says important colored and white folks are getting mighty angry. They say Pumpsie deserves a chance.

tices with Team

# PUMPSIE GOES TO FARM TEA

# Sports

# AT FENWAY

WE WANT A
PENNANT
NOT A
WHITE TEAM

Did Pumpsie
Get a Bad Deal?

Most Fans
Want Green

E GOAL
NS GAME

Finally one sticky July day, my prayers are answered. The Sox tell him, "Pumps, pack your bags. You made it."

They are playing a night game in Chicago. We huddle around the radio. Mama makes popcorn to make it feel like we're at Fenway. We listen real hard, but we don't hear Pumpsie's name.

"Maybe he'll come in later," Papa says, smiling, when he sees our long faces. The game enters the fifth, sixth, and seventh innings and still no Pumpsie. Now Papa's expression changes.

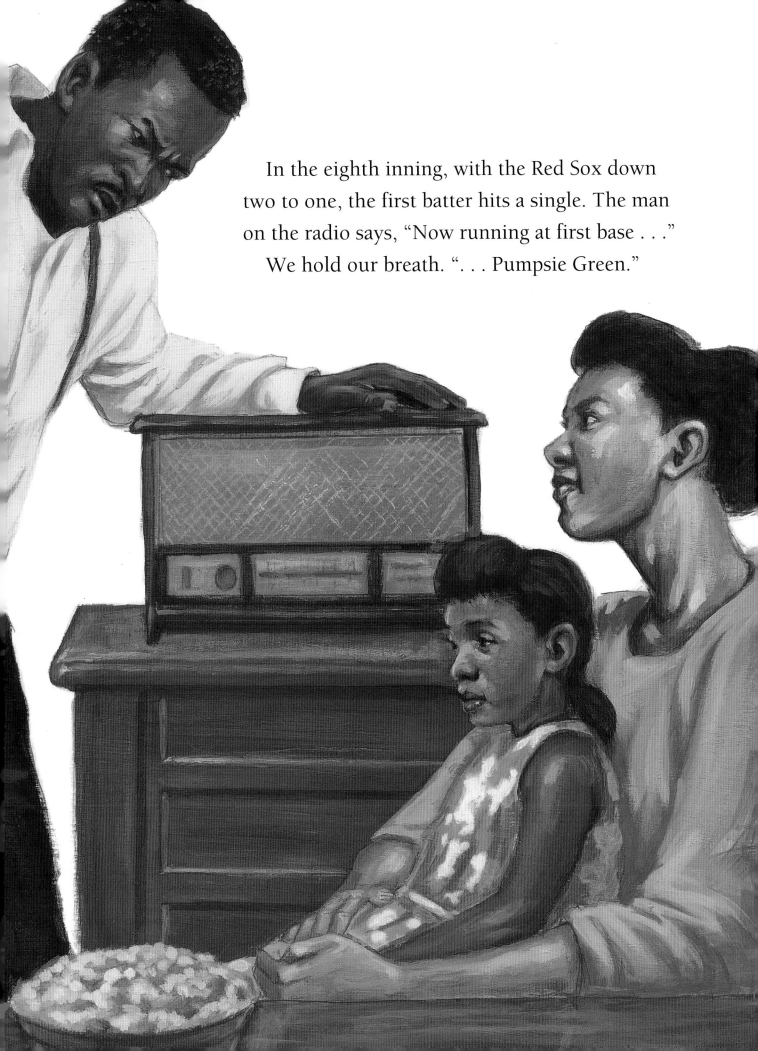

In the eighth inning, with the Red Sox down two to one, the first batter hits a single. The man on the radio says, "Now running at first base . . ." We hold our breath. ". . . Pumpsie Green."

"This is history!" Mama shouts.

"Do not forget this moment!" Papa roars, wiping his eyes. "Never, ever, ever!"

"We promise!" Lisa and I hug Mama and Papa like we just won prize money.

I imagine Pumpsie taking a lead, rocking back and forth to distract the pitcher like Jackie Robinson used to do.

The Sox make one, two, three outs. Pumpsie is stuck at first. No luck.

We lose. Again. I'm not kidding.

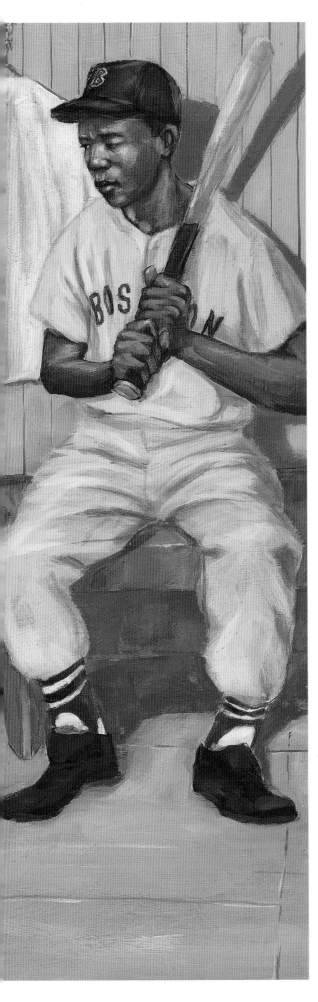

The next day there's a picture in the newspaper of Ted Williams giving Pumpsie batting tips. I figure that if "Teddy Ballgame" wants to be Pumpsie's friend, maybe the Sox can start winning.

The Red Sox play away games in Kansas City, then Cleveland, and finally Detroit. Whew!

The night they land in Boston, newspapermen push and shove at the airport to snap pictures—*POP! POP! POP!* It's like Pumpsie's a movie star.

The next morning at breakfast, Papa surprises us.

For once, the stands are packed with colored faces.

In the first inning Pumpsie heads to his position at second base. I hear a man yell, "Get that Negro off the field!"

Mama tells us to ignore him. "Some people have hearts full of ignorance," she explains.

Pumpsie makes a nifty pivot for a double play that ends the top of the first. Now it's Boston's turn to bat.

"Leading off for the Red Sox—number twelve, Pumpsie Green!" The announcer's voice echoes through Fenway. We're stomping our feet so much, the stadium starts to shake.

Pumpsie takes two practice swings. He digs in. The pitcher looks for his sign. He shakes his head. Then the pitcher winds up. Pumpsie pulls his bat back. The ball shoots out of the pitcher's hand like a rocket. Pumpsie swings.

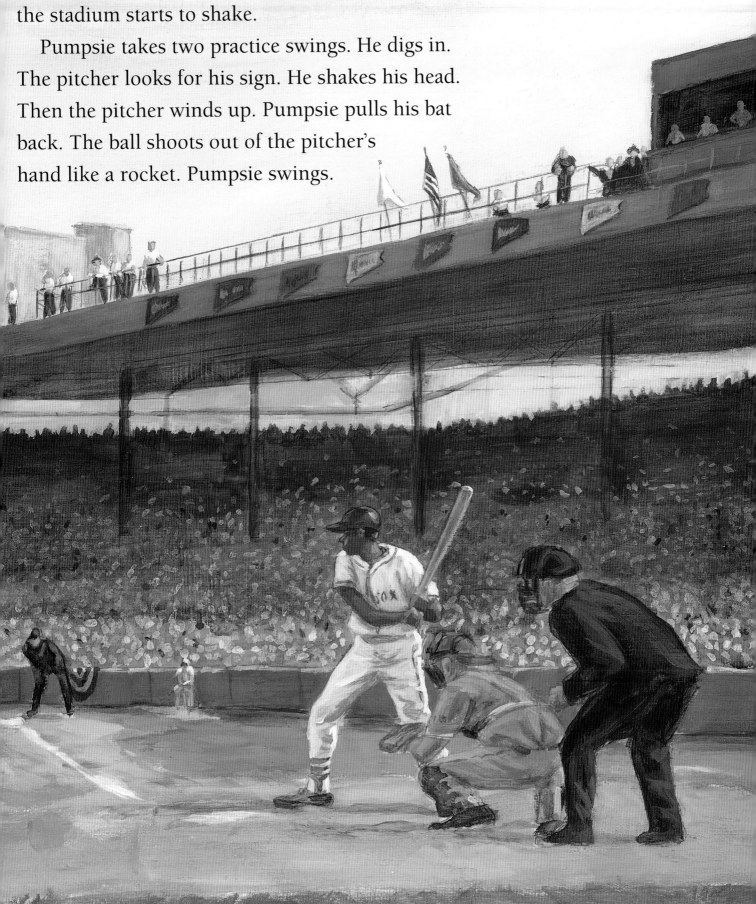

*WHACK!* The ball climbs higher and higher. I think it's going to make it over that mean Green Monster.

No! It clanks off the top of the wall and bounces back onto the field. Pumpsie rounds first base and runs like his own uniform can't keep up. The outfielder heaves the ball back in.

Pumpsie slides. Safe at third!

Fenway goes crazy. I look over to where the man full of ignorance is sitting. He's gone! Lisa and I whoop even louder.

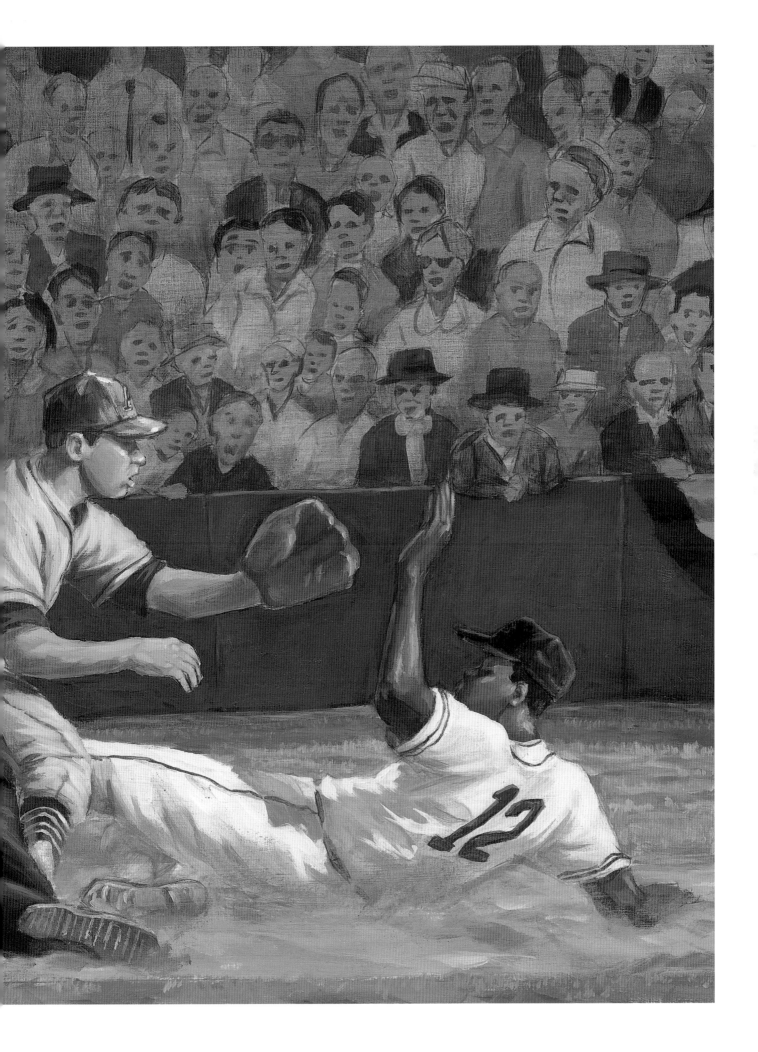

The Sox win. After the game, I stop walking
for a minute and turn around. I look at Fenway
and the crowd and tell my eyes to take a picture.

The bus is buzzing real loud on the ride back to Roxbury. People are asking if the Sox can get back into the pennant race now that we have Pumpsie. That gets me thinking: Is he as good as Jackie?

We pass people standing in front of stores and on lawns. They're waving Red Sox flags and holding up that newspaper picture of Ted and Pumpsie. I can even hear chants of "Pumpsie! Pumpsie!" and car horns beep, beep, beeping.

It's like New Year's Eve and Fourth of July rolled into one. I'm not kidding.

One day I'll tell my kids how long we waited
for Pumpsie Green. I'll tell them how he dug his
heels into the batter's box. I'll tell them how I
pretended it was me, Bernard, sliding into third.
And I'll tell them it happened at
Fenway Park, the most beautiful
place in the world.

*Finally*. Just like Mama and
Papa said it would.

# AUTHOR'S NOTE

**Bernard** is a fictional character, but the events leading up to Pumpsie Green's 1959 arrival in the major leagues with the Boston Red Sox are true.

I was Bernard's age when I first heard of a baseball player with a funny name—Pumpsie Green. By that time it was 1963, and his short career was quickly coming to a close with my favorite team, the New York Mets.

Unlike Bernard, I didn't think very much about racism in baseball while I was growing up in the 1960s. Jackie Robinson broke the color barrier on April 15, 1947, at Ebbets Field as the first African American major-league ballplayer with the Brooklyn Dodgers. That's what I knew, and I assumed that every team integrated quickly after that.

Sadly, that's not how it happened. I was shocked when I learned that it was another twelve years before the Red Sox allowed a person of color to wear their uniform. Many said the Sox did it only because public opinion was growing more vocal and determined each day. Both fans and civil-rights organizations were becoming increasingly angry that the Red Sox wouldn't let a black player play.

Think about it this way: by the time Pumpsie was called up from the minors to play for the Sox, Jackie had already been retired for two years!

Many people—especially younger fans— aren't familiar with this history. There's not very much out there to read about Pumpsie Green. The Red Sox sometimes invite him back to Fenway to throw out a ceremonial first pitch. To some that seems like a nice gesture. To others it might feel a little embarrassing, because it's a reminder of a time when the Sox management didn't do what most people in society thought was the right thing.

Bernard's story is about more than baseball, the game. It's about moving toward equality and how sports can help change society for the better. For kids like Bernard who lived through Pumpsie's debut in 1959, seeing the last Major League Baseball team racially integrated was an important personal and historical moment.

# SOURCES

Booth, Clark. "About Pumpsie Green and the Indelible Stain Yawkey-Era Racism Left on the Red Sox." *Dorchester Reporter*, July 23, 2009. **www.dotnews.com/columns/2009/about-pumpsie-green-and-indelible-stain-yawkey-era-racism-left**.

Bryant, Howard. *Shut Out: A Story of Race and Baseball in Boston.* New York: Routledge, 2002.

Nowlin, Bill. *Pumpsie & Progress: The Red Sox, Race, and Redemption.* Burlington, MA: Rounder, 2010.

Tygiel, Jules. "Baseball Has Done It." In *Baseball's Great Experiment: Jackie Robinson and His Legacy,* 328–32. New York: Oxford University Press, 1983.

ELIJAH "PUMPSIE" GREEN SHORTSTOP

You can find a list of the first black players on each major-league team by searching online.